FOXES
IN A FIX

ALSO BY W. BRUCE CAMERON

Bailey's Story

Bella's Story

Cooper's Story

Ellie's Story

Lily's Story

Max's Story

Molly's Story

Shelby's Story

Toby's Story

Lily to the Rescue

Lily to the Rescue: Two Little Piggies

Lily to the Rescue: The Not-So-Stinky Skunk

Lily to the Rescue: Dog Dog Goose

Lily to the Rescue: Lost Little Leopard

Lily to the Rescue: The Misfit Donkey

W. BRUCE CAMERON

LILY
TO THE rescue

FOXES
IN A FIX

Illustrations by
JAMES BERNARDIN

A TOM DOHERTY ASSOCIATES BOOK
NEW YORK

LILY TO THE RESCUE: FOXES IN A FIX

Copyright © 2021 by W. Bruce Cameron

Illustrations © 2021 by James Bernardin

All rights reserved.

A Starscape Book
Published by Tom Doherty Associates
120 Broadway
New York, NY 10271

www.tor-forge.com

The Library of Congress Cataloging-in-Publication Data is available upon request.

ISBN 978-1-250-76272-6 (trade paperback)
ISBN 978-1-250-76279-5 (hardcover)
ISBN 978-1-250-76273-3 (ebook)

Our books may be purchased in bulk for promotional, educational, or business use. Please contact your local bookseller or the Macmillan Corporate and Premium Sales Department at 1-800-221-7945, extension 5442, or by email at MacmillanSpecialMarkets@macmillan.com.

First Edition: September 2021

Printed in the United States of America

0 9 8 7 6 5 4 3 2 1

Dedicated to the kindhearted folks of the Humane Society of Indiana, saving lives since 1905.

1

The smells coming in through the open window of the car were cool and clean. They told my nose that our car ride was taking us to a place called "Up in the Mountains."

Dad was in the front seat of the car, and I was in the back with my girl, Maggie Rose. Her skin smelled sweet, with another odor I thought of as "soft." Her lap was a sweet, soft place.

Maggie Rose leaned forward to speak to

Dad. "It's funny, it was so warm at home and it's so cold here."

"That's because we're so high up," Dad explained. "The air's thinner up here, and it can't hold the heat."

"Bighorn sheep!" Maggie Rose exclaimed, pointing out the window. "Look, Lily! On that rock, see?"

I looked, but there were no dogs and no squirrels, just a lot of big animals with curly

horns on their heads, standing around on a big rock as if they were stuck. Dogs can always think of something fun to do, even on a rock. But not these creatures. They looked ready to stand there all day.

"Why does Mr. Martin live way up here?" Maggie Rose asked. "There's hardly anybody around."

"I think that's the point." Dad chuckled. "He used to be a pilot, so he spent his life in airports and big cities all over the world. Now he just wants peace and quiet."

Maggie Rose stroked my back. "Does he at least have a dog?"

Dad smiled sadly. "He had one. But it had to be put to sleep last spring."

"Oh," Maggie Rose said. She hugged me tightly and put her face in the fur on the back of my neck. "I hate hearing that," she mumbled.

Dad nodded. "I know, hon. Dogs don't live

forever. So we have to love them while we have them, don't we?"

Maggie Rose lifted her face. "I know what we should do. Let's invite Mr. Martin to come down to Mom's rescue and get a new dog!"

"Oh, I've mentioned it before," Dad replied. "He always says he's not ready."

My girl was quiet for a moment, then brightened. "Once he meets Lily, he'll realize he needs a dog for sure!"

Dad nodded. "Might work."

My girl grabbed my face with both hands. "Okay, Lily, you need to be on your very best behavior. Your job is to convince Mr. Martin he *has* to have a dog."

I felt I was being told something very important, and hoped it had to do with bacon.

The car bumped a few times and then stopped. We were here!

Where was "here"?

Maggie Rose opened the door, and I jumped

out and drank in the odors. "Here" was trees and a cold breeze and big looming hills and wet, muddy ground. We headed toward a wooden cabin. A man walked out onto the front porch.

"Hello, James," he called. "Is that you, Maggie Rose? You've gotten so big! Are you in college now?"

My girl laughed. "Third grade!"

A new friend! I charged over to run up the steps and put my feet up on the man's legs to sniff him. He smelled of coffee and some kind of salty cheese.

"Friendly little thing, isn't she?" the man said.

"Lily," my girl wailed. "You got muddy paw prints all over Mr. Martin's pants!"

"Oh, that's all right," the man answered. I wagged at him. Would he be willing to share some of that cheese with a certain good dog?

Maggie Rose and Dad climbed up the

steps. "Hi, Mark. It's been too long!" Dad greeted him.

"That it has," the new man agreed. "Come in. Nice to have company."

We all started in through the open door, but my girl pulled on my collar. "Lily," she said, "remember, you have to be a *good dog*!"

I wagged. I love being called a good dog by my girl.

Inside the cabin I sniffed for food crumbs. The grown-ups sat down on chairs near a big window to talk. People like to do that.

Maggie Rose walked over to see what the books on a bookshelf smelled like. I joined her. Sadly, they smelled like books. "Mr. Martin?" she called. "Did you make these model airplanes?"

The new man—he was probably "Mr. Martin"—looked over at us. "Sure did. Those are all of the planes I flew."

"Wow," Maggie Rose said.

"You can pick them up if you want," Mr. Martin offered.

Maggie Rose carefully pulled something off the shelf and studied it. Then she leaned down to show it to me.

I sniffed it. It was a plastic toy! I lunged and grabbed it.

Maggie Rose gasped. "Lily!"

I backed away and my girl followed. Time to play Chase-Me! I dashed around the couch and she followed. "Lily!" she called frantically.

I raced across a rug and it bunched under my paws. Maggie Rose tripped over it and grabbed at a lamp, which fell over with a *thump*. I spat out a piece of the toy and jumped onto a chair, sending some pillows flying, then leapt over a coffee table and ran back to shake the toy in Maggie Rose's face.

Instead of trying to grab the toy so we

could both pull on it, Maggie Rose snatched at my collar. Then she pulled the toy right out of my mouth. It seemed like she had forgotten how to play Chase-Me.

Dad came over to help pick up the lamp and the things that had fallen off the coffee table. "Sorry about that, Mark," he said.

"I'm so sorry," my girl added. She leaned

down to whisper in my ear. "Would you *please* be a good dog? It's *important!*"

I loved the feeling of her breath in my ear.

"No harm done," Mr. Martin said. "I can easily glue that propeller back on."

"Lily's usually such a good dog," Maggie Rose told him.

I wagged. Yes, I was a good dog. I was also an expert at spotting squirrels—and I could see one right now, hopping in the backyard. I barked in joy and dove forward.

Crash! My face hit a window that I hadn't noticed. A wet smear painted the glass.

The squirrel was still there, only a few feet away. It was holding a pine cone in its mouth. It didn't seem to care about me at all. I barked in frustration.

"Lily! No!" my girl said sharply.

From her tone of voice, I could tell she had not seen the squirrel.

Mr. Martin laughed softly. "I'd forgotten

what it's like to have a dog. They can be quite a handful!"

My girl's shoulders slumped.

Mr. Martin took a sip from his mug. "All right, James," he said. "So what's so important you had to come all the way up here to tell me in person?"

D ad took a swallow from his mug and then set it down very carefully. Maggie Rose went back to the bookshelves but didn't hand me another toy.

"So what if I told you I had a job for you, flying animals to Alaska, and it pays zero, plus you'd have to buy your own gas?" Dad asked Mr. Martin.

Mr. Martin laughed. "Well, that sounds great."

"You know my wife's a vet. And she does some work with the zoo. They've been breeding rare species there, trying to get the population numbers up," Dad said. "They've been so successful with their Arctic foxes, they're ready to release some in the wild."

My girl looked up sharply. I stared at her alertly. Had she finally seen the squirrel? Could we go and chase it together?

Mr. Martin nodded. "Ah, okay. So that's why you need to fly to Alaska."

"Thing is, we don't have much budget. It's for a good cause, but you'd be donating everything," James finished.

"Can I go with you, Dad? Please? Can I?" Maggie Rose blurted out.

Dad was watching Mr. Martin. "We don't know if we're going yet, Maggie Rose."

Mr. Martin laughed. "That's not playing fair, you know. How can I say no to that face? Sure, why not?"

Maggie Rose clapped her hands. "Yes!"

Dad and Mr. Martin laughed and then went back to talking while my girl leaned down to me. "We're going on a trip, Lily! An adventure!"

I wagged at my name because my girl was excited. That always makes me happy.

Maggie Rose leaned closer and spoke even more quietly. "Now we just have to talk Mr. Martin into getting a dog." She picked up something from the shelf that did not smell like a toy. She held it out toward Mr. Martin. "Is this your dog?" she asked him.

I heard the word "dog" and looked around, puzzled. Was there another dog somewhere?

"It is," Mr. Martin said. "That's Bruno. He was a good dog."

"Mom has lots of new dogs down at the rescue," Maggie Rose said. "Wonderful dogs. You should come and pick one out."

Mr. Martin shook his head. "I don't think so, hon."

"But why not?" Maggie Rose asked.

Mr. Martin sighed. "Well, I'm not sure I'm ready. And it would be hard to find the right kind of dog for this place. We're really only free of snow for a couple months in the summer. Bruno was a Bernese mountain dog, and he loved the snow. But it's not every dog who can be happy up here."

They were both saying "dog" a lot, so I couldn't imagine why they both seemed sad. Maybe it was because Maggie Rose kept picking up things that were not toys. And then she did it again! She picked up a flat, square thing and held it out to Mr. Martin. "Who's this boy?" she asked.

Mr. Martin smiled. "Me!" he said. "And that's my very first dog."

They were happier now, even though Maggie Rose was still picking up not-toys. People

are so much harder to understand than dogs.

"What's wrong with his leg?" Maggie Rose asked.

"Just born that way, with only three legs," Mr. Martin answered. "But it didn't bother him any. He could run and play just like any other dog. We called him Trip."

Dad chuckled. Mr. Martin grinned. I

thought Maggie Rose seemed a little confused. She put the flat not-toy back down on the shelf.

I trotted back to the window to see if the squirrel was in the yard. But it wasn't. I'd done my job and scared it away.

I scratched at the glass anyway.

"Can I let Lily out?" Maggie Rose asked Dad.

"Sure."

Maggie Rose slid the door open and I plunged out into the cold air and down the steps to the ground. I hurried over to some trees to see what there might be to sniff. The ground was cold and wet, squishing under my feet.

There was something else back there— the rotting body of a very large bird that had been dead for some time. It smelled *wonderful*. After sniffing it up and down, I dropped a shoulder and rolled in the delicious odors. My fur soaked up water from the muddy ground.

"Lily!"

My girl was calling me. I jumped to my feet, wagging, and then raced up to the sliding doors. Maggie Rose stood back to let me into the house. "Lily! You're all muddy!" she cried.

I shook the water out of my fur and my girl blinked as the droplets hit her. Then she raised her wet hands to her face. "What's that *smell*?"

Dad jumped to his feet. "She's rolled in something dead. Ugh."

Mr. Martin stood up as well. "There's a utility tub in the mud room. I'll get some old towels."

Dad picked me up, which I usually like. But then he carried me to the back of the house and put me in a small bathtub.

What was he doing? We'd been having so much fun! Surely there wasn't going to be a bath for such a good dog!

Well, there surely was. My girl soaped me

17

and rinsed me and dried me with towels. "Lily," she moaned sadly. "You're doing everything wrong. Mr. Martin will never want a new dog now."

I understood exactly what was going on. She had given me a bath, and of course it made her sad. It made *all* of us sad.

She kept me wrapped in towels and sat with me in her lap on the couch. I didn't feel much like running around anymore.

"I don't think I'd have the energy for a new dog," Mr. Martin said with a smile.

"But Lily is normally such a good dog! She keeps me company, she sleeps on my bed— she's my best friend in the world."

Mr. Martin nodded. "I felt the same way about my dog Trip—when I was a boy, we did everything together. And Bruno, he was the best friend a man could have."

I heard a buzzing and Dad dug a phone out of his pocket. "I'd better take this. It's my wife."

"Of course," Mr. Martin said.

Dad talked to his phone, which is something people do all the time, even if there is a good dog in the room willing to listen. But then he straightened in surprise. "You've *got* to be kidding me. No. Of course. We'll drive straight there. See you soon." Dad turned and shook his head.

"What's wrong?" Mr. Martin asked.

"Looks like our trip to Alaska might be off," Dad replied grimly.

3

Everyone stared at Dad, so I did, too.

"Why, Dad?" my girl demanded. "What's wrong?"

"Your mom just got a call. They were backing up a truck to transport the Arctic foxes, and the brakes went out. It crashed right through the fence. The foxes escaped," Dad replied.

"Oh, no!" Maggie Rose exclaimed.

"No" is not my favorite word. But I could

tell that my girl was not saying it to me, so I didn't mind it this time.

"Can they get very far?" my girl asked.

"No idea," Dad said with a shrug. "But in the snow they'll be practically invisible. My wife says it's really coming down in town."

"That means it'll be a blizzard up here pretty soon," Mr. Martin observed. "You'd better get going. These mountain roads can be dangerous."

We took another car ride. I could smell that we were headed toward snow, and I could tell that my girl was unhappy.

I love snow, but I do not like it when Maggie Rose is sad. "I really wanted Mr. Martin to be impressed with Lily so he'd want to get a dog," she said gloomily. "But Lily, you barked and jumped on the furniture and broke his model airplane and you rolled in something horrible. Horrible, Lily! That was bad!"

I heard the word "bad" and my name. But I hadn't been bad, had I?

Maybe Maggie Rose was disappointed in me because I hadn't been able to catch the squirrel. But that hadn't been my fault. Nobody had opened the door!

Dad chuckled. "Some things don't work out as planned."

"We just got in a Great Dane puppy at the rescue," Maggie Rose said. "He's so cute—Mr. Martin would love him!"

"I'm sure he's adorable, but a Dane isn't really a snow dog. And speaking of snow, we're driving right into the storm."

I watched alertly as some black arms began waving back and forth across the car's windshield. No one in the car waved back.

"I know! What about the new cockapoo? Mom says they're a good breed for snow."

"Well, your mom's the expert. But in the mountains there are coyotes and bobcats and foxes. If Mark's going to get a dog, it needs to be a big one, so predators will leave it alone."

Maggie Rose slumped in her seat. I nosed her hand.

"Would you rather go with me to search for the foxes or be dropped off at home?" Dad asked.

"Oh, no, Lily and I want to help catch the foxes!"

Dad chuckled again. "That's my game warden girl. I just hope they stay on the zoo grounds."

"Lily could find them, I'll bet," Maggie Rose boasted.

I wagged at my name.

"Your mom'll take all the help she can get."

"What happens if they get out of the zoo?" my girl asked.

Dad frowned. "That'd be very bad. There wouldn't be anything for them to eat in the city, and they don't know about cars. I think we'd lose some of them. They're just babies."

"Then we have to find them!" Maggie Rose declared. She turned to me. "Lily, it's up to you to find the foxes!"

When we stopped, I could tell where we were by the odors. It was a place called "Zoo" and nothing smells quite like it, because of all the animals who live there.

My girl opened the car door. I was surprised to see Mom and Bryan and Brewster getting out of another car, right next to us.

Bryan is Brewster's boy and Maggie Rose's brother. I trotted over to them because my nose caught the scent of something good. Sure enough, Bryan had turkey treats in his pockets. And his pockets smelled like peanut butter, too, because his hands had been in them. Bryan's hands always smell like

peanut butter. It's one of the things I like most about him.

I was surprised to see Brewster at Zoo. I come to Zoo a lot, because I have friends to visit here. But Brewster has never been. He probably came for the turkey treats.

Brewster and I sniffed each other behind our tails. He didn't smell any different back there than he usually did.

"Brewster's part hound dog, so he can help track the foxes!" Bryan declared.

Dad and Mom looked at each other. "I thought, why not?" Mom said.

Dad shrugged. "Fine by me."

"And Lily will make friends with them and bring them out of wherever they're hiding," Maggie Rose added confidently.

Brewster shook himself. He seemed annoyed at the thick white snowflakes landing on his fur. I was coated with the same white stuff, but it didn't bother me. I was too happy and excited to be bothered. I love Zoo!

A man came hurrying toward us. He had a thick, puffy jacket on and a hat pulled down low. I remembered his smell from previous visits. His pants were usually dusty and full of interesting smells, so I dragged Maggie Rose over to him.

"Dr. Quinton, how are you?" Mom said.

"Worried!" replied Dusty Pants as I jumped

up to put my wet paws on him. "Lily, yes, hi, I'm glad to see you, too. Chelsea, James, thanks so much for coming. Hello, Maggie Rose. Hello, Bryan."

"This is Brewster," Bryan said. "He's a senior dog."

"Is it all right that we brought the dogs?" Mom asked. "We hope they can help."

The man nodded. "It is. All the zoo animals have been put inside—some were already there, obviously. Our tropical animals don't like this kind of weather. So the dogs won't be a problem."

"Brewster has tracking blood in him," Bryan added.

We all walked through a gate into Zoo itself, a place with lots of small paths that branch off here and there through bushes and trees. Usually there are delicious things on the ground at Zoo—squashed French fries and melting blobs of ice cream and sticky clumps of cotton candy. But today I couldn't find any treats like that. The snow covered up anything tasty that might have fallen.

Bryan took Brewster off the leash. "Find the foxes, Brewster!" he commanded firmly.

Maggie Rose did the same for me. "Lily, find!" she told me. "Foxes, Lily. Find the foxes!"

I wondered what a "foxes" was. Was it a game? Something to eat?

Brewster put his nose down into the snow and sniffed. Then he set off as if he knew exactly where he was going.

"It's working!" Bryan exclaimed.

4

We all seemed to be playing a game called Let's-Follow-Brewster. That was okay with me! I ran along behind him. Big flakes of snow fell on my face, and I kept blinking to keep them away from my eyes.

Brewster didn't seem to care about the snow at all. He just headed straight toward a building with a set of steps up to a door.

"He's got the scent!" Bryan said excitedly.

There was a door at the top of the steps.

Brewster stood by it and gave Bryan an expectant look and waited.

"That's my office," Dusty Pants said as he climbed the steps. "I don't think the foxes could possibly be in there."

He opened the door. Brewster headed in. I trotted up the steps to see Brewster shake snow from his fur, look around, spy a couch in a corner, and hop up for a nap.

All the grown-ups laughed.

"Sorry, Bryan," Dad said. "Doesn't look like Brewster had the fox scent after all."

"Oh, Brewster, you silly nap dog," Maggie Rose said.

"I don't think he understood what we wanted him to do." Bryan sighed.

Dusty Pants smiled. "I don't mind if your old hound stays in my office, son. But we need to get back to looking for the foxes."

"How long have they been gone?" Dad wanted to know.

"More than two hours, I'm afraid," Dusty Pants replied. Dad and Mom exchanged worried glances, and the man nodded. "Of course, we were worried that the truck might have hit one or two of them when it went through the fence. We were so busy checking under the truck that we didn't even think that they might head for the hole in the fence. By the time we figured it out, it was too late."

"They're naturally curious animals. And if they made it through one fence . . ." Mom sounded worried.

Dusty Pants nodded. "If they leave the zoo, we'll lose them for sure."

It seemed like we were all going to stay and watch Brewster take a nap, but then the people changed their minds. We left Brewster in the room with the couch and headed back out into the snow.

I loved bounding through the cold, white stuff and shaking it off my fur. Maggie Rose hurried behind me, scuffling through the snow in her boots. She kept saying the word "foxes," and I still wasn't sure what a foxes was, but I guessed I'd figure it out sooner or later.

We were walking past a building with giant windows in one wall when I stopped and stared. Behind the glass, a large snake lifted its head to look at me.

I've met snakes before. They never want to play, and usually glide away before I can even sniff them properly. But I'd never seen one as big as this. It was as thick as Maggie Rose's arm, and it didn't seem to have any mouth at all, just two round dark eyes that watched me closely.

I gazed back just as closely. Then I jumped up to put my front paws on the glass. I dropped down into the snow with my front legs low and my rear end high. I was ready to play, if this snake wanted to!

The snake wiggled, too. Then it did something amazing. It floated up into the air!

I jumped back and barked, and just then I spotted an animal behind the snake, a strange one with a big head and two enormous, flapping ears. It was bigger than a horse. And one thing I know about horses is that they are too big to play with. I backed away.

The flying snake seemed to be clinging to the giant animal's face in some odd way. In fact, I was beginning to understand that it

wasn't really a snake—it was a part of the big
not-horse.

"Oh, Lily," Maggie Rose said. She giggled.
"That's a baby elephant. He's nice and warm
in his house, but we're not looking for ele-
phants, okay, Lily? We're looking for Arctic
foxes."

One of the reasons I love Zoo so much is all
the strange, new animal smells. This huge
not-horse with the snake on its face carried

a rich odor, along with the tangy scent of straw. I inhaled deeply, learning the smell in case I ran into it somewhere else. Maybe it would come to our house sometime. Maybe it would like to curl up for a nap with me in my girl's bedroom.

Maggie Rose was impatient. "Come on, Lily. Let's find the foxes!"

Was the strange not-horse a foxes? Perhaps, but Maggie Rose didn't seem very interested in it. She hurried me away.

Maggie Rose and I had a nice walk in the snow. She seemed distracted, though, and kept looking under bushes or behind trash cans as if she'd lost something that would be good to eat.

I tried to help her, even though I wasn't sure what we were looking for. I sniffed along the snowy ground and noticed that some other animals had been there before me. Their footprints had been covered up by the fresh snow, but I could still tell that they'd run along this way.

They weren't animals I'd ever met before, I knew that. Their odors were new to me. I kept my nose down, tracking them.

Maggie Rose was looking under a big bush. I left her there and followed the scents. They led to a gap in a fence. I squeezed through.

I saw that I was in a sort of yard. There were two big metal machines, like oddly shaped trucks, parked in a corner. Near them a huge hole had been dug in the earth. I like to dig holes, but this one was much bigger than anything I could dig on my own. Even if Brewster was helping me, we couldn't dig something like this. And of course, Brewster probably wouldn't help dig—he was much more interested in lying on the couch with his eyes shut.

Everywhere I saw piles of rocks. There were long, thin logs of wood stacked up against one of these piles. A small, white face with bright black eyes was peering at me from around that stack of wood!

A friend!

5

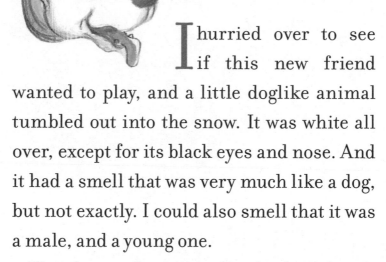

I hurried over to see if this new friend wanted to play, and a little doglike animal tumbled out into the snow. It was white all over, except for its black eyes and nose. And it had a smell that was very much like a dog, but not exactly. I could also smell that it was a male, and a young one.

The almost-dog jumped up high in the air and landed in the snow. I didn't jump, but I flopped down on my belly and wagged. Two more of the almost-dogs had come out from behind the woodpile. I could smell that they were littermates of the young one who was still jumping.

When they took off running, leaping on each other, I was excited to join them. Chase-Me! We were playing Chase-Me! They darted about, turning so quickly I kept falling behind.

The one male I'd first met kept jumping up into the air and landing on all four feet—I thought of him as Jumper. Jumper and I were soon playing Wrestle, and the others joined in. They all smelled like young males, and they were very good at playing. They knew Chase and Wrestle and Jump, but none of them soared as high as Jumper.

We raced in a circle and crouched and leapt on each other and ended up in a big wrestling pile, gently gnawing paws and faces and whatever else ended up in our mouths.

I was panting at the same time that I was shivering in the cold. This was so much fun!

When I wiggled out of the pile, I glanced around and sniffed. I had a feeling that I was being watched, and sure enough, I could smell more almost-dogs nearby. But it was hard to spot them with snow landing on my eyelashes.

I shook the wet out of my eyes and spotted a couple of white almost-dogs watching alertly from the top of the woodpile.

Just then I heard Maggie Rose calling my name. "Lily, where are you? Lily, come!"

I am a good dog who knows what to do when I hear "Come." It meant leaving my new friends, but Maggie Rose is my girl. I wiggled out through the gap in the fence and found my girl standing with her hands on her hips.

"There you are, Lily!" she said as I ran up to her. "Where did you go? We're supposed to

be looking for the foxes. Oh, Lily, you're cold. You're shivering!"

My girl loves all animals, so I knew she would like my new almost-dog friends. I wagged up at her and then turned and trotted back through the snow to the hole in the fence. I wanted her to come and play with us.

Maggie Rose didn't understand my invitation. "Come on, Lily!" she said, taking off at a run. I galloped after her. It felt less like

Chase-Me and more like Come, though. And Come is not as much fun as Chase-Me.

I was glad when we climbed up some steps. Maggie Rose pulled open a door and a blast of warm air came out. We were back in the room where Brewster was still taking a nap. After a few moments, I stopped shivering.

Mom and Dad and Bryan were there, along with Dusty Pants and a few other people. I could tell he was very worried about something. "No tracks?" he asked.

"Just really difficult, with it snowing this hard," Dad explained.

"We checked around the fox's habitat, where the truck broke down the fence," Mom said. "No sign of them."

"I searched near the big cat area," Bryan said.

"Lily and I looked where there's a bulldozer," Maggie Rose added.

"Bulldozer? Oh, I know where you mean," said the new man. "That's where we're expanding the home for the polar bears. I know you were trying to help, but polar bears hunt Arctic foxes. They're natural enemies. The foxes wouldn't be anywhere near there. Much too dangerous."

Dusty Pants walked restlessly around the small room. Brewster lifted up his head, laid it back down, sighed, and closed his eyes again. Dusty Pants turned to Mom. "Do you think they've left the zoo grounds?"

"We have to hope not," Mom replied.

"It's getting late," Dad added. "It's been hard enough to try to see a bunch of white animals during a snowstorm in the day—it will be impossible at night. We should pack it in, get a fresh start in the morning."

"Come on, Brewster. We're going home," Bryan said.

Brewster followed us to the open door, but when he saw us step out into the snow he sat down.

"Come on, Brewster," Bryan repeated.

Brewster gave me a glum look. He is a dog who does not like snow.

After we waited for Brewster to step out into the snow and Brewster kept on not doing it, Dad picked him up and carried him to the car. Brewster seemed very content. He'd be happy to have Dad carry him everywhere we went.

The next morning was another day Brewster wouldn't like.

"Bryan and I are going to head out and see if we can make money shoveling people's decks and sidewalks," Craig announced at breakfast. I listened carefully but did not hear anything about feeding Lily toast.

"Maggie Rose, we'll drop you at the rescue,

and you and Lily can help Gretchen there to-day," Mom said.

"But Mom," Maggie Rose protested. "I want to go with you and Dad and help look for the foxes!"

Mom and Dad looked at each other. Dad smiled. "That's my game warden girl," he said.

"All right," Mom agreed. "Dr. Quinton said that today he'll take the staff to hunt for signs of the foxes outside of the zoo, but your dad and I are going to search inside the zoo grounds. As long as you stay close to us, you can come along."

"Hear that, Lily?" my girl asked me. She still wasn't talking about toast, but I could hear the excitement in her voice. "We get to go! But this time, no wandering off. We need to find the foxes!"

6

Back to Zoo! A few flakes of snow were still falling down through the air, but not as many as yesterday. My girl clapped her mittens together. "Time to find the foxes, Lily!"

"Find the foxes"? I still didn't know what "foxes" meant. But I was very excited to go back and play with my almost-dog friends. I darted off, heading for their yard, but my girl called me back. "No, Lily, stay close to me. We have to find the foxes!"

Maggie Rose didn't put my leash on me, but I still stayed close to her side. I had to, because whenever I decided to follow an interesting scent, she called me back.

After a while, we found our way to where we'd been the day before. The scent of the almost-dogs drifted on the wind along with the snowflakes. I looked up at Maggie Rose and wagged hard. She must have brought me here so we could all play together!

But she didn't go into the yard. Why not? She kept saying that "foxes" word to me. She was still busy playing Find-the-Foxes.

"That way is the polar bear exhibit," my girl told me. "I'll bet you they love this weather!"

I stared up at her and then looked hard at the gap in the fence. But she didn't understand what I meant, and she didn't go in there to play.

"Maggie Rose!" I heard Mom call from

back in the direction of Brewster's nap room. "Don't go too far!"

"I'm not!" my girl shouted.

"Come on back this way!" Mom urged loudly.

"Okay," my girl muttered. She put her hands in her pockets and trudged toward Mom's voice.

She hadn't said "Come" to me. And the scent of the almost-dogs was so strong—I couldn't help myself! I slipped through the gap in the fence. I would just visit with my friends for a few moments, and then I would go back to be with my girl.

The almost-dogs were playing Chase-Me in the yard. Jumper started leaping with excitement when he saw me, and before long I was doing Wrestle with all of them, rolling and twisting in the snow. I tried jumping up and landing on all my feet like they were doing, but didn't see how that was much fun.

Then I noticed a couple of large males

heading over to a fence made of tall iron
bars. Curious, I followed to see what they
were doing.

Two adult almost-dogs slipped between two
of the bars and scrambled up a short wall.
On the other side of the wall was a round,

snow-filled field. It was much lower than the ground where I stood, as if someone had dug a deep hole, put a yard in it, and surrounded it with a rough stone wall.

My friend Jumper shot past me and through the bars. Wherever the adults were going, he wanted to go, too.

My attention, though, wasn't on the almost-dogs. I was gazing with amazement at two enormous creatures who were in that deep-down yard.

They weren't as big as the animal with the snake stuck to its face, but they seemed nearly that size. Like the almost-dogs, they were covered from ears to tail in dense white fur, and their eyes and noses were black. They walked like dogs, but their feet were the size of dog bowls and were tipped by enormous, scary-looking claws.

A growl rose in my throat, but I didn't bark. Jumper and the two adults had scrambled over the wall. Now they sprang to the snowy ground. They were in the yard with the huge beasts!

What were they doing? I could tell from up here that the huge creatures were dangerous. They had their heads down to food dishes, and their wicked, sharp teeth tore at the meat there. They looked as though they could eat an almost-dog in one bite!

Jumper followed the two adults as they slunk along the base of the wall. They hadn't yet been seen by the big creatures.

I did not know what to do. The almost-dogs didn't seem to understand that these beasts were not the sort of animal you'd want to play with. But that seemed exactly what one of the adults meant to do.

While the other two almost-dogs hung back, the biggest one, a male, darted forward. When the huge beasts lifted their heads, he froze, not moving.

A whimper escaped my lips. Jumper needed to get out of there!

One of the giant animals stopped feeding and took a slow, careful step toward the adult male almost-dog. He didn't move. I was so worried I started panting.

The second big creature joined the first. Now they were both coming

closer to the male. And he still wasn't moving! Why didn't he run?

Jumper and his friend, meanwhile, were inching forward in the snow. They were leaving the biggest male not-dog to face the advancing hunters by himself.

"Lily!" I heard my girl call.

I tensed. I knew I needed to go to her. But I couldn't, not with my new friends in such danger!

Both of the huge beasts charged forward at once. I saw the male almost-dog run at last. He turned this way and that, zigzagging across the snow, just like Jumper had when he was playing Chase-Me. The huge hunter slashed through the air with his wicked claws. He missed!

"Lily!" Maggie Rose called again.

To my amazement, Jumper and his friend darted forward, straight to the food dishes! They snatched up big hunks of meat and dashed away to hide by a large log that was lying up against some big rocks.

But the big male almost-dog was now running right at the stone wall around the yard. He jumped, scrabbling at the wall with his claws, but he couldn't climb it. He fell back into the snow, with the wall behind him and the two giant hunters facing him.

He was trapped!

I couldn't help myself. I barked, putting a frantic note of fear in my voice.

The sound seemed to startle the huge beasts. They turned their heads to stare up in my direction, as if they had never heard a dog bark before.

"Lily! Where are you?" I heard my girl call. I could tell by her voice that she had heard me. A good dog would go to her, but I couldn't. My new friends were all still trapped in the yard by the giant creatures with the deadly claws!

7

Jumper and his adult
friend didn't stay hid-
den under the log that was propped up against
some rocks. Instead, they scampered up it, the
big chunks of red meat dangling from their
jaws.

They bounded from the log to the stone
wall and were on top of it in a moment.
They turned to look back down at their male
friend, who was still trapped.

I barked again, but the fierce beasts were

no longer interested in me. They turned back to the other almost-dog in front of them.

I yipped in surprise as the almost-dog ran right at the giant beasts. He dodged between them, zigzagging back and forth.

One of the hunters lunged and missed, and now the almost-dog was running for the log. The hunters followed, but every time they were close, the almost-dog darted off in a new direction. The bigger animals were slower to turn. They couldn't keep up!

The almost-dog leapt up on the log and raced toward the wall. One hunter growled and slashed at him with her deadly claws, but it was too late. He was already at the top of the wall, joining his friends.

I wagged in relief. Jumper and his friends squeezed through the fence and scampered through the snow to the woodpile. Several almost-dogs came out from behind it. In a

moment they were all sharing the meat that Jumper and his friends had brought.

I licked my lips. It was so nice for the almost-dogs to slip into that down-deep yard and escape from the giant hunters so we could all have a delicious meal together. I hurried over to join my friends.

But when I got close, all of the almost-dogs darted into their den, except for Jumper. He leapt high and I caught the wonderful scent of the red meat on his lips as he turned and dashed off for Chase-Me.

I hesitated. Wouldn't it be better if we had a little snack first?

"Lily! Come!"

In all the excitement over the dangerous beasts and the wonderful food, I had forgotten about my girl. Guiltily, I turned away from Jumper's invitation to play.

"Lily!" Maggie Rose stood at the fence, near the gap where I had wiggled in. I ran over to sniff her and wag at her through the bars. The almost-dogs might have forgotten to share their food, but my girl was sure to pull something good out of her pocket for me to eat.

I could hear Mom's voice now as well. "Maggie Rose, where are you?"

"Over here!" Maggie Rose called out. "I think Lily got stuck behind a fence!"

I glanced over my shoulder. Jumper had vanished with the rest of his friends. They were all hiding. I decided to wiggle out through the gap in the fence to join my girl, but she stopped me. "No, Lily. Stay. You might get hurt by the wires."

I have learned Stay, but I don't always remember what it means. Still, when my girl stretched out her hand to block the hole in the fence, it was clear that she wanted me to remain in the yard with the meat and the almost-dogs.

I did a good Sit in the snow and hoped for a treat.

"Oh Lily, you're shivering again! It's too cold for you!" Maggie Rose exclaimed.

Mom and Dad soon appeared behind Maggie Rose and stood looking at me through the bars of the fence.

"I'm worried that if she tries to come out she could get hurt on the sharp edges," Maggie Rose said.

"Good thinking," Mom told her.

Dad reached down to the hole I had crawled through and bent back the wires. "Come now, Lily."

First Stay, then Come. I was certainly being asked to do a lot of things without any treats.

That's how it is with humans, sometimes. They'll hand out all sorts of delicious snacks when they are first teaching a dog what to do. But as soon as the good dog has mastered something like Lie Down, people will say the command but forget to give a reward.

I lowered my head and went through the fence to Dad, since he had said "Come."

"Did anybody find the foxes yet?" my girl asked.

Both Mom and Dad shook their heads. "Dr. Quinton is beside himself," Mom replied.

"There are no tracks anywhere. The snow filled them all in."

"I figure that they went exploring, looking for food," Dad added. "They're going to be disappointed. They mostly feed on fish and rodents, but in this weather they're not going to find either."

"What will happen to them?" Maggie Rose asked.

Dad gave her a grim look. "I can't imagine them surviving. Some local foxes can live in urban areas—they avoid people and eat garbage and small animals—but these particular foxes need to live on the tundra. That's really the only place they can catch their prey."

"We have to find them!" my girl declared.

"We tried, Maggie Rose," Dad said sadly. "But it looks like they've escaped, and we're not going to have any luck until someone looking out their window sees a skulk of white foxes—a skulk is what you call a group of foxes."

"Time to go home," Mom said.

"We need to get your dog warmed up," Dad added.

I knew what Home meant. It meant a car ride and then being with Maggie Rose on her bed. I turned for a last look at the log pile, thinking of my new friends and the meat they were hopefully saving for me . . . and I saw Jumper! His head was sticking up over the pile of logs, and he was watching me.

"Let's go, Lily," my girl said as she followed Mom and Dad away from the fence.

I didn't want to leave without a goodbye bark. At the noise, two more little heads popped up. They were as curious about the noises I could make as the big, dangerous beasts had been.

I decided that every animal at Zoo would

be better off if they knew what a barking dog sounded like. So I did it again.

Maggie Rose had turned back. "Lily?" she said. She looked past me and her eyes widened. "Mom! Dad! I see the foxes!"

8

ood dog, Lily!" my girl praised. Mom and Dad came rushing up to see what a good dog I was.

I wagged happily. I like being a good dog. Though I wasn't sure what, exactly, I had done that was so good.

"Where?" Dad asked urgently.

Maggie Rose gave a hop of excitement. "There. See? In that woodpile. They're peeking over the top!"

Mom and Dad and Maggie Rose were now staring at the place where the almost-dogs had gone to hide. The people must have caught the scent of that meat. I wagged with joy. If we all went to the hiding place, I would for sure be getting a treat! People can reach into refrigerators and pull out turkey—it would be so simple for one of them to stick a hand in a stack of logs and come out with food for Lily!

But that's not what happened. "I'll get the nets," Dad announced. He turned and ran toward Brewster's nap house, the snow flying up behind his boots.

Mom crouched down next to me. "Lily found the foxes!"

There was that word again. I yawned anxiously, thinking that if Mom and my girl were going to start talking about that, we might lose track of the chunks of red meat. And it was very important that I get some! Hadn't

I helped the almost-dogs get the food away from the savage hunters with the huge claws?

"I am so glad we brought you two with us this morning, Maggie Rose. Your dad is right. You really are a game warden girl!"

When Dad returned, he brought several people with him. I decided it was going to be one of those times when humans are very busy doing things that make no sense to dogs, and dogs just have to wait until their people are ready to play again.

Dusty Pants played with a chain and then a gate swung open. All of the people, including Dad, ducked into the yard with the almost-dogs. "Stay with Lily," Mom said as she followed them.

I never thought Stay applied to anybody but me and sometimes Brewster. But now Maggie Rose was not moving, as if she was expecting Mom to return with a treat.

I watched with interest but no understanding as two people carefully lifted the logs off the stack. The rest of the people stood in a circle with nets draped in their arms.

Then I realized what they were doing—they were removing the logs so they could get to the red meat and give me some! How nice of them!

There was Jumper! He dashed away from the logs that were left, right into one of the nets. Then he lay there squirming while the woman holding the net picked it up off the ground. Then another almost-dog, and another—soon the wood stack was gone and all of my friends were in nets and I realized that they had eaten all the meat without leaving me any.

"Well, that's all of them," Dusty Pants said. "Thanks to you two, they're safe."

"Thanks to Maggie Rose," Dad corrected. "She was the one who saw the foxes."

"And thanks to Lily! I wouldn't have looked if she hadn't barked," Maggie Rose added.

"Lily is welcome in this zoo any time she wants to come," Dusty Pants told us. I heard my name but didn't know what they wanted from me.

"You found the foxes, Lily!" my girl told me as we followed the people. "Good girl to find the foxes! But you're so cold!"

We climbed into the car, which was toasty warm. I curled up with my girl.

"There were traces of meat in that wood-pile," Dad remarked.

"So the foxes were able to hunt?" Mom replied, surprised.

Dad shook his head. "There were tracks to the polar bear habitat. Looks like they were in there, stealing food."

"From the polar bears?" Maggie Rose asked. "Isn't that really dangerous?"

"Yes, but they do it in the wild anyway," Dad replied. "They're brave little critters."

"Does this mean we're going to take a trip

to the North Pole after all?" my girl asked Dad.

Dad chuckled. "Well, not all the way to the North Pole, but far enough north that trees don't grow. Yes, I'll call Mark Martin when we're back at the house."

"How is Mark?" Mom asked as I yawned sleepily.

"He needs a dog," Maggie Rose told her.

Dad laughed. "Maggie Rose is like you, Chelsea," he told Mom. "She's determined to get people to adopt a pet, no matter what."

"I'm proud of you for that, Maggie Rose," Mom said.

Maggie Rose smiled, stroking my head. I could feel the shivers leaving my body in that warm car. "We're going to Alaska, Lily!" she whispered to me.

We did a car ride home from Zoo, and I took a nap. I was worn out from all that playing in the snow. Brewster had a nap, too. He was worn out from sleeping all day.

A few days later, Mom hugged my girl and Dad, and Brian and Craig said "See ya," and we drove to a parking lot—a very big one, wet with melting snow.

Maggie Rose put me on my leash and took me to a very strange, long car. There was a set of steps that led up to a door in the car's side. "Come on, Lily!" Maggie Rose said, and she started up the steps.

I hesitated. I didn't like the look of those steps. They were steep and a little damp and slippery. Maggie Rose came back down and, grunting, carried me up.

I licked her cheek. I love my girl.

Inside the strange car the air was flooded with the smell of almost-dogs. When Maggie Rose set me down I tracked the odors past some seats to a big crate that had been

fastened to the floor. Inside the crate were
my friends!

I could tell they were anxious, and wondered
if this was their first time in a car. They were
either sitting and staring or pacing restlessly.

When I poked my nose at one of the holes
in the crate, Jumper came right over to me.
He made a low, moaning sound followed by a
yip. I wished I had some way to tell him that
car rides were almost always fun. Maggie

Rose would roll down a window and we could watch out for squirrels and other animals.

But all of the almost-dogs were tense and a little afraid. I thought they would be happier if they weren't in the crate, so I was excited when my girl knelt down next to me to let them out!

9

But to my surprise, Maggie Rose did not reach for the door to the crate. She did not let my friends out to run around in the car. Instead, she put her mouth close to my ear.

"Now remember, Lily, your job is to convince Mr. Martin that he needs a dog," she whispered. "Be a real good dog this time, okay?"

I wagged. I loved being a good dog.

"Aren't they cute? Do you like the foxes, Lily?"

There was that word again—foxes. Was Maggie Rose telling me that the word for an almost-dog was "foxes"?

"All right," someone called as he climbed up the narrow steps. It was Mr. Martin, followed by another man. "Everybody ready?"

Dad and Maggie Rose sat in the car seats behind where Mr. Martin and his friend strapped themselves in. I curled up by her side. "Lily found the foxes, Mr. Martin!" Maggie Rose called out sunnily.

"That so?" he replied.

Suddenly, the car made a loud noise—a *huge,* very, very loud noise—and began moving. I gazed up at my girl in alarm. Something was wrong! Car rides were never this loud. I felt pressed down onto the floor, as if a giant hand were holding me there. But there was no hand! I barked.

"No, Lily!" my girl said.

No? The pressure and the noise were even worse, and I did the only thing that made sense, which was to throw my head back and howl.

"Lily! Stop that!" Maggie Rose scolded. "You'll upset the foxes!"

I heard "foxes" and glanced back to see that my friends looked as miserable as I felt. I howled some more.

"Is your dog all right?" Mr. Martin yelled over the roar of the car.

"Yes!" my girl called back. She reached down and put her hand around my snout. *"Please,* Lily. Please be good!"

I heard words I recognized, but did not understand what she was trying to tell me.

My girl unsnapped the belt across her lap and threw her arms around me. Being held by Maggie Rose is the most wonderful feeling in the world. I stopped howling.

"It's going to be a long flight, Maggie Rose," Dad said. "We'll stop a few times for fuel. You should try to get some sleep."

"I'm too excited to sleep! We're up so high!" she responded.

After a while the feeling of being held down went away and I became used to the noise, but it was still the strangest car ride I have ever been on. For one thing, nobody opened a window. And when I jumped up on a seat to look out through the glass and spot squirrels, I saw *nothing*. The entire outside was gone!

I barked again when we hit something hard, and Maggie Rose put her hand on

my snout. Then we all climbed down those narrow metal steps for me to squat in some bushes, and then we went back into the strange car. Once again the pressure and the noise made me howl.

After a while, Mr. Martin unsnapped his lap strap. With his head bent over, he made his way back to talk to us. "I'm sorry about Lily making all that noise, Mr. Martin," my girl apologized. "She's never been on a plane before."

"That's all right," Mr. Martin replied. "Amazing she could howl for so long, though."

Maggie Rose nodded sadly. Then she frowned. "Um, don't you need to be flying the plane?"

"Lou can handle it," Mr. Martin said. "That's the whole point of having a copilot— we can each take over for the other."

"So . . . are you thinking at all about getting a new dog?" she asked eagerly.

I perked up my ears, because my girl

sounded excited and she'd said the word "dog." I looked at Mr. Martin and wagged.

Mr. Martin shook his head. "To tell you the truth, I'd forgotten just how much energy a young pup can have. I might be too set in my ways for that."

Sometime after that, I jumped up into my girl's lap. She yawned and then curled up and shut her eyes. Dad brought us a blanket and I cuddled into it, close to my girl.

I like naps by myself and naps with Brewster, but naps with Maggie Rose are the best naps of all.

I was still mostly asleep when the strange car hit something *again*. My girl's eyes snapped open.

"We're here," Dad told her.

The car bounced and jolted over a very rough road, finally coming to a stop. Maggie Rose stretched and then we all climbed down to the ground.

I looked around. We were in another gigantic parking lot. What was the point of such a long, strange car ride if the place we were going was only another parking lot? We could just as well have stayed in the first one!

I raised my nose. The air was clean and cool and moist. I smelled trees and water. It reminded me of the place called Up in the Mountains.

Mr. Martin's friend waved goodbye to us and walked off. The rest of us went in a different direction, to where a man was waiting for us in a car. "This is Nick. We went to college together," Dad said. The man, Nick, hugged Dad and shook hands with Mr. Martin and nodded at Maggie Rose and patted me.

"So appreciate you volunteering your services," Nick told Mr. Martin.

"Flying is my passion. And I wanted to help the foxes out of their fix!" Mr. Martin replied.

We took another car ride, and it was by far the better one. The outside was back, and I could see it through the window, which my girl lowered a little bit for me. We drove to a big house with lots of windows.

I was immediately excited when we jumped down out of the car. My nose told me there were dogs here. Many, many dogs!

I didn't have time to search them out, because we all went inside the big house. I followed Dad and my girl down a hallway to a room. Dad put a box with a handle and a zipper on a bed. Maggie Rose pulled on the zipper and opened the box.

"I have a surprise for you, Lily," my girl said.

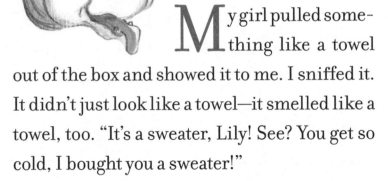

10

My girl pulled something like a towel out of the box and showed it to me. I sniffed it. It didn't just look like a towel—it smelled like a towel, too. "It's a sweater, Lily! See? You get so cold, I bought you a sweater!"

It was, apparently, a sweater. She seemed awfully excited, which I thought was a little odd, because a sweater was nothing more than a towel with holes in it. But then she knelt down and played Tug with each one of my legs, and when she was finished, the sweater was hugging me tightly.

I sat and looked up at her, hoping she'd take this sweater thing off me. I wanted to follow my nose to all the dog smells I'd picked up on the way into this big house, not sit around with a strange towel clinging to me.

"You look so cute! Come on, Lily!"

I followed her back down the hallway. My tail stuck out of a hole in the sweater and I did not wag.

Mr. Martin and Nick and Dad all turned and smiled at me. I thought maybe one of them might help me out of the sweater. "Well, look at that," Mr. Martin said. "You sure look silly, Lily."

My girl looked troubled. "Lily gets cold easily because her fur is so short."

Mr. Martin nodded. "Makes sense."

"But there are plenty of dogs who don't get cold at all," Maggie Rose added firmly. "Like the huskies outside in the pen. Can Lily go play with your dogs, Mr. Cooper?"

My girl called Dad's friend "Mr. Cooper" because she didn't understand that his name was Nick.

"Oh, no, that wouldn't be a good idea," said Nick. "They're sled dogs, and they're bred to work. They're not going to want to play, especially with a strange dog wearing a sweater. They might even hurt Lily if she goes running up to them."

He reached down to pet me.

"Oh," my girl replied in a quiet voice.

"Tell you what, though. I've got some dogs who would love

to meet Lily," Nick told her. "One of my females had a litter about eight weeks ago. Want to see some puppies?"

Maggie Rose became very excited, so I wagged. That's what I do, make fun things even more wonderful by adding a little wagging tail to the action.

We followed Nick down a different hallway to a different room. Dad came with us. In the room we met a mother not-sweater dog and a lot of not-sweater puppies.

"They're adorable!" my girl exclaimed.

"Hardly anything cuter than a husky puppy," Nick agreed.

The puppies all charged me at once while the mother dog looked on calmly. Instantly I was in the middle of a pile of wrestling pups. When several of them snagged my sweater with their sharp little teeth, my girl unsnapped it off of me, and then we really had fun!

Maggie Rose laughed and cuddled the puppies as they crawled onto her lap and then off again to play some more.

"Look, this one has something wrong with his foot!" Maggie Rose said, bending close to a puppy in her lap. She rolled the pup over onto his back. He wiggled and nibbled her fingers.

Nick, who was sitting near the mother dog, nodded. "Yep, we don't know exactly why, but he was born without his right front foot. So he doesn't really use that leg, but he gets around on the other three pretty well. And you have to admit, he's darn cute."

"He's wonderful," Maggie Rose said. She hugged the puppy close.

Nick nodded. "Can't be a sled dog on three legs, though."

"So what's going to happen to the little fellow?" Dad asked.

Nick shrugged. "I know a guy who reclaims auto parts who wants a dog to chain up to protect the place at night."

Maggie Rose glanced up. "So he'll be all alone in a junkyard all night?"

Nick smiled at her. "This part of the world, the dogs all have jobs, Maggie Rose. There's no use for a dog who can't work."

I did not know why my girl suddenly seemed sad, especially with a puppy in her lap and a dog like me giving her a lick on her cheek.

Nick stood. "Well . . . ready to take the foxes to their new home?"

I was excited to leave the big house and go back out into the snow-filled yard, but I was not excited when my girl put me back in the sweater. Worse, she kept me on a leash, so I wasn't able to run over to the huge pen and visit all the big, furry dogs who lived there.

The dogs did not wag, did not bark, did not seem friendly at all. Their stares were as cold as the frosty air.

I am a dog who can make friends with anybody. I have crow friends and pig friends and a leopard friend. But I did not think these dogs wanted to be friends with me.

I blamed the sweater.

Nick and another man carried the crate full of foxes over to a long skinny car that lay flat on the ground. It had no wheels and no sides and no top. I followed my girl and Dad to another such car.

Then I watched in amazement as Nick and his friend let the silent dogs out of their pen. The dogs were excited as they were hitched up to long leashes. Were we all taking a walk? If so, why was my girl holding me still as we sat down in the car with no wheels?

"Ready for a sled ride, Lily?"

I did not know what Maggie Rose was asking. I spotted Jumper in his crate with his foxes friends. He was not wearing a leash and did not look excited.

Nick stood up in front of our car. "Line out!" he yelled.

I watched with no understanding as the other dogs formed a straight line, standing in their leashes.

"Mush!" Nick shouted.

To my amazement, the silent dogs lunged

forward on their leashes. Dragging a person on a leash is considered bad dog behavior in my family. But when these dogs pulled hard on their leashes, our car started to move and everyone seemed happy about it.

"Here we go!" Dad cried.

11

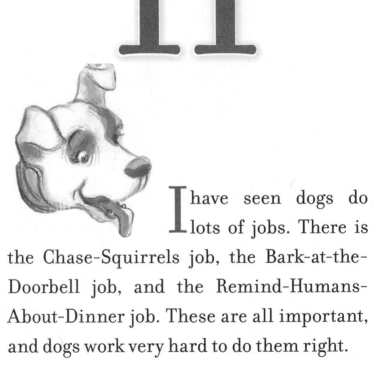

I have seen dogs do lots of jobs. There is the Chase-Squirrels job, the Bark-at-the-Doorbell job, and the Remind-Humans-About-Dinner job. These are all important, and dogs work very hard to do them right.

The dogs on leashes apparently had the job to be Bad. They threw their whole weight into the harnesses, and they yanked as if they were pulling us toward a very delicious dinner. No one yelled "No." No one was unhappy with them.

Nick's friend stood in the other open-air car, and the two men talked to the dogs, calling out words I didn't understand.

What sort of place was this, where it was fine for dogs to yank on their leashes, and a good dog like me was forced to wear a sweater?

"Dad," Maggie Rose said. She seemed unhappy, and I nuzzled her hand.

"What's wrong, Maggie Rose?"

"I don't want that little puppy to live on a chain in a junkyard. He's sweet and loving and cute," my girl said firmly. "If Mr. Cooper is going to just give him away, why can't we take him? Take him back to the rescue and find a good home for him?"

Dad gazed back at her, but didn't answer.

I wondered why my girl kept saying "Mr. Cooper." At first, I thought it was because she thought that was Dad's friend's name, and no one told her it was actually Nick. But now I wasn't so sure.

There were no trees. The ground was flat and mostly snow-covered, and the wind came to my nose from far, far away. Soon we came to the top of a very low hill and I saw a large lake with a rocky shore and chunks of ice floating in the still water. Dad turned and grinned. "This place is perfect!"

How could he be so happy with dogs yanking on their leashes? I did not understand.

"Gee!" Nick and his friend yelled. The dogs turned us toward the lake. I do not like swimming, and hoped that wasn't what was coming next.

"Whoa!"

We stopped. The leashed dogs were panting. Nick's friend gave them water.

Nick came over to us. "There's a small

skulk of foxes living around here. Plenty of lemmings come down to the water, and there are large colonies of voles nearby, so they have a good food source."

"It's great," Dad replied.

"Why aren't there any trees?" Maggie Rose wanted to know.

"It's called tundra," Dad explained. "The air is too cold and the growing season is too short for anything but a little grass and moss. The foxes are going to love it here!"

I watched curiously as Nick and Dad carefully picked up the crate with the foxes and carried it down toward the lakeshore. I saw Jumper glance at me and wagged at him. I didn't really understand what was happening, but I knew if Dad was involved, everything would turn out just fine.

The two men set the crate down and opened the door. "All right!" Nick said. Both of them ran back up to us. They were very happy.

"How long will they stay in the crate?" my girl wanted to know.

Dad shrugged. "They feel safe in there. Eventually, curiosity will get the better of them, but right now, they obviously don't want to go exploring."

I yawned. The air was very cold, but for some reason I wasn't shivering.

We sat in silence. I could smell the foxes and I could smell the leash-yanking dogs, who were lying down, still attached to one another by their leashes. Finally, they were being good dogs.

And there was another odor on the air, dank and strong. I lifted my nose to it. I had never smelled anything like it, though it reminded me of the huge beasts at Zoo, the ones with the fierce claws. This smell wasn't the same, but it was similar.

"Oh, no," Nick said softly.

"What is it? What do you see?" Dad asked.

Nick pointed. "There. See?"

Dad's shoulders slumped. "Oh, boy."

"What is it, Dad?" my girl asked anxiously.

Dad gave her a grim look. "See up there on that small rise? Where there's no snow? He's not moving now, so you can barely make him out. He's dark with white markings."

"Is it a badger?" Maggie Rose guessed.

"Close. It's a wolverine," Dad replied. "One of the fiercest animals on the planet. Worse, wolverines hunt Arctic foxes, especially young ones."

"Oh," Maggie Rose replied in a small voice. "No wonder they don't want to come out of their cage."

"That's right," Nick agreed. "They know he's there."

"Does he know about the foxes?" Maggie Rose asked.

"Wolverines have amazing noses," Dad answered. "He knows they're there, all right. He just doesn't understand about the crate. But if one of them tries to make a run for it, his instincts will take over." Dad gazed sadly at my girl. "I'm sorry for what you're about to see, Maggie Rose."

"What do you mean?" Maggie Rose asked. Her voice made me look up at her, worried. What was wrong with my girl? "We have to do something!"

Then my gaze returned to the animal with the strong odor, because it had moved down the slope toward the crate. It kept stopping to raise its head. It was about the size of Brewster, but it was not a dog. It smelled fierce and wild.

"We can't do anything," Nick replied unhappily. "Wolverines are very rare. We can't interfere."

"But he'll hurt the foxes!" my girl protested. "It's not fair. They're stuck in the cage!"

"Maggie Rose," Dad said gently. "This is just one of the things we have to accept. We have to let nature take its course."

My girl was so upset that tears were slipping down her cheeks.

This was a day I could not understand. I didn't understand why the leash-yanking dogs were allowed to misbehave. I didn't understand what we were doing out here in the cold, or why my foxes friends were sitting, not moving, in the crate. I didn't understand why I was wearing a sweater.

But I did understand that my girl was frightened and sad. And I did understand that the odd, Brewster-sized not-dog was the reason she felt so bad.

There was only one thing I could do.

12

I lunged to the end of
my leash, and, with
all the anger I could muster, I barked at the
new, wild animal.

A dog always knows what's going on with
other dogs. I could feel the leash-yanking
dogs react to my fierce barking.

"Lily," Dad murmured.

All the dogs, still leashed together, rose to
their feet and joined their voices with mine.
I wasn't even sure they knew what we were

barking at, but they matched my fury with their own. Together, we made a loud chorus of dogs.

For a moment the wild creature froze. Then, with an odd, hopping gait, it turned and fled up over the hill, vanishing from sight.

We all kept barking, because once you've started it's a little hard to stop.

Nick turned to Dad. "A wolverine is too tough to care about a single dog, but a dozen dogs . . . that's a different story."

"We let nature take its course," Maggie Rose added happily. "It was natural for the dogs to bark."

"You're right, Maggie Rose," Dad replied.

"Lily thought of it first!" My girl beamed.

After what seemed like a long time, an adult foxes slipped out of the crate, followed moments later by the rest of them. I saw Jumper bringing up the rear. He spotted me and leapt up into the air, full of joy. But he didn't pause as he followed his friends. They all ran away across the snow, heading in the opposite direction from the wild, Brewster-sized not-dog.

I had been through this sort of thing before, making friends with animals before

they ran off to live somewhere else. They didn't know how soft and sweet Maggie Rose's bed was, so they didn't know what they were missing. I thought I saw Jumper turn and give me a last look before he vanished into the snow, but I couldn't be sure. His scent lingered for a while longer.

The leash-yanking dogs started with their bad behavior again, and they did it all the way back to the big house. There Maggie Rose unstrapped the sweater from my back and I played with puppies.

One of the little dogs spent most of the time in my girl's lap. "Oh, puppy, just because you are missing a foot doesn't mean you should live in a junkyard on a chain. You deserve a much better life," she whispered.

Dad and Nick came to see me playing with the little dogs. "Time for bed, Maggie Rose."

"Mr. Cooper," Maggie Rose said, "I know that up here all the dogs have to work, but my mom runs an animal shelter, and we can find this little puppy a home with people who will love him. Could we take him back with us? Please?"

Nick looked at Dad. Dad looked at Nick. They both looked at Maggie Rose.

"How can I say no?" Nick replied.

The next morning we returned to the big parking lot. We all climbed back into the strange car where nobody opened windows. I could still smell the foxes.

I wasn't the only dog in the car. The puppy who ran a little oddly was joining us! We immediately started to do Wrestle, which was the right thing to do. An older dog like me is supposed to teach a younger dog how to behave.

When the car roared and the squishy, heavy feeling settled over me, I could tell the little puppy was scared, so I didn't howl. I lay down next to him and offered comfort. Soon the heavy feeling went away, and we started playing again.

I have been around a lot of puppies, so I wasn't surprised when suddenly he sprawled out on the floor and fell asleep. That's just how they behave at that age. I took a nap myself, but we both woke up when Mr. Martin came back to visit us.

Mr. Martin scooped the puppy up and grinned at him. He held the puppy close and let him lick his face.

I saw Maggie Rose smile.

On that car ride, Mr. Martin spent a lot of time playing with the puppy—even more than I did. When the puppy became tired, he curled up in Mr. Martin's lap and closed his eyes, relaxed and happy.

Mr. Martin was this puppy's person, I realized. Just like Bryan was Brewster's person and Maggie Rose was mine. A dog can always tell.

"Cute little guy," Mr. Martin said.

"That he is," Dad agreed.

"We'll find him a good home," Maggie Rose chimed in.

Mr. Martin gazed down at the puppy in his lap, a thoughtful look on his face.

"Of course, it's always hard to find a home for a three-legged dog," Dad observed carefully.

Maggie Rose nodded. "That's right. Most people think it will be too much trouble. You need to know what you're getting into."

"This little guy gets along just fine," Mr. Martin said.

"Sure does," Dad agreed.

"He'll be happy in Colorado, too," Maggie Rose said. "He's a husky, so his fur will be thick to protect against the snow."

"And huskies grow to be pretty big, even wolf-like," Dad added. "So he wouldn't be happy to be a city dog. He needs lots of room to run."

"Good thing we live so close to the mountains!" Maggie Rose declared.

Mr. Martin raised his eyes, but he still had the soft smile he'd been wearing as he gazed at the puppy sleeping in his lap. "If I didn't know better, I'd say you two were hinting at something."

Dad laughed and Maggie Rose beamed a bright smile.

"Is there an adoption fee?" Mr. Martin asked quietly.

Dad just shook his head. "You volunteered your time and fuel for the Arctic foxes. The rescue isn't going to charge you a thing."

"You're going to be so happy with your new puppy!" Maggie Rose exclaimed.

After a few moments, Mr. Martin put the puppy down and went back to sit at the front of the car. The puppy collapsed back into a nap. I curled up around him, feeling a little like a mother dog.

I get to know a lot of animals. Some of them have to go and live somewhere else after we've been friends for a little while. This happened to a skunk I once knew, and some baby geese who thought I was their mother, and two pigs. And, of course, Jumper and the rest of the foxes were that sort of friend, too.

Dogs are often different, though. Some,

like Brewster, stay a part of my life. And others go off with their people. I didn't know if I would be playing with this nameless puppy after our car ride was over, but I did know he would be going off to live with Mr. Martin in Up in the Mountains. They were meant to be together.

Every person needs a dog.

And every dog needs a person.

MORE ABOUT ARCTIC FOXES

Arctic foxes live on the tundra, the land near the North Pole where trees do not grow.

Arctic foxes hunt rodents, birds, and fish, and may eat berries and steal eggs from nests. They will also steal food from kills made by polar bears, wolves, and wolverines.

An adult male fox is called a dog. A female is a vixen.

Young foxes are called kits. A vixen usually has four to eight kits at a time, but she may have as many as twenty.

A fox lives in a family group with a mother, father, and kits. Sometimes one of the female kits will stay with her parents an extra year and help to look after her younger brothers and sisters.

A fox may weigh between six and a half pounds (about the size of a chihuahua) and seventeen pounds (about the size of a pug).

The soles of an Arctic fox's feet are furry. This keeps their feet warm in the snow.

Arctic foxes live in burrows that may have a hundred entrances and exits.

An Arctic fox's fur changes with the season. Some are white in the winter and brown in the summer. Others are pale gray in winter and darker gray in summer. Either way, they stay camouflaged in winter snow or summer dirt.

Arctic foxes are hunted by polar bears, brown bears, wolverines, wolves, red foxes, and eagles.

A fox will wrap its bushy tail around its body to keep itself warm.

READ ON FOR A SNEAK PEEK AT
LILY TO THE RESCUE:
THE THREE BEARS,
COMING SOON FROM STARSCAPE

Y ou get to see Freddy today, Lily!" Maggie Rose sang to me. I wagged because she was happy and because I recognized the name "Freddy." Freddy is a sleek ferret who sometimes sits in a cage at Work. Freddy is my best ferret friend. Actually, I don't know any other ferrets, but if I did, Freddy would be my favorite.

I was still wagging when we walked in the door at Work. Instantly I could smell that Maggie Rose's two brothers were already here, along with Brewster.

Brewster is a dog who lives with us and sleeps on Bryan's bed. He was napping on a dog blanket near the door and raised his head as we came in. I gave him a polite sniff.

"Hey, Maggie Rose," Craig said. He was lugging a heavy bag that smelled of wonderful dog food. "Bryan's outside in the back, playing with two puppies we just rescued."

"Puppies!" Maggie Rose said.

Craig nodded. "I'm almost done stacking dog food, and then I'll come out, too."

My girl ran to the back door and I dashed after her. I didn't know what we were doing, but I was excited to be doing it. It seemed that we were not going into the room of cages where Freddy was waiting for me. That was too bad. But whatever we were doing must be more important.

It wasn't important enough to wake Brewster from his nap, though. Almost nothing can do that.

We burst out into the sunshine and I smelled Bryan and two puppies.

"So cute!" Maggie Rose exclaimed.

One puppy was covered with shaggy dark fur, and one was white with big dark spots. Of course, they were impressed and amazed to see a good dog and her girl.

They ran to me, tripping over themselves. I let them jump on me and chew at my face until Shaggy bit down too hard. Then I flipped him over on his back.

It's the job of older dogs to teach younger dogs how to play properly.

"I've named them Biker and Slam," Bryan told my girl.

Maggie Rose sat on the lawn and the puppies broke away from me and climbed into her lap. She giggled and picked up the spotted one, kissing him on the nose. I trotted over and shoved my face into my girl's face for my own kiss.

Craig came out the back door. There was still no sign of Brewster.

"Those are the worst names ever, Bryan," Maggie Rose told him.

"What are?" Craig asked, falling to his knees and reaching out to the shaggy puppy. Shaggy began chewing Craig's fingers.

"Slime and Blinker," Maggie Rose answered.

Craig hooted.

"That's not what I said!" Bryan responded. "Biker and Slam."

"What? Are you crazy?" Craig answered. "Slacker and Bam?"

"I'm not talking to either of you," Bryan muttered. I saw he was trying not to grin.

I looked up and wagged as Mom came out to see us. She smells different every day. Today she carried the odor of cats.

Craig rose to his feet. "What's wrong, Mom?"

ABOUT THE AUTHOR

W. BRUCE CAMERON is the #1 *New York Times* bestselling author of *A Dog's Purpose*, *A Dog's Journey*, *A Dog's Way Home*, *A Dog's Promise*; the young reader novels *Bailey's Story*, *Bella's Story*, *Cooper's Story*, *Ellie's Story*, *Lily's Story*, *Max's Story*, *Molly's Story*, *Shelby's Story*, *Toby's Story*; and the chapter book series Lily to the Rescue. He lives in California.

Don't miss these

LILY TO THE RESCUE

adventures from bestselling author

W. BRUCE CAMERON

Go to BruceCameronKidsBooks.com
for downloadable activities.

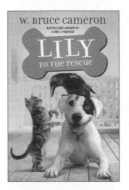
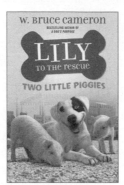
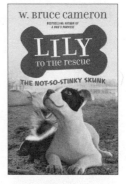
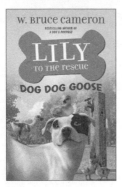
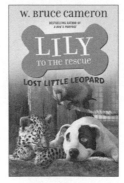
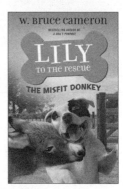

Interior art credit: Jennifer L. Meyer